STEM

Paper Airplanes

Composing Numbers 1–10

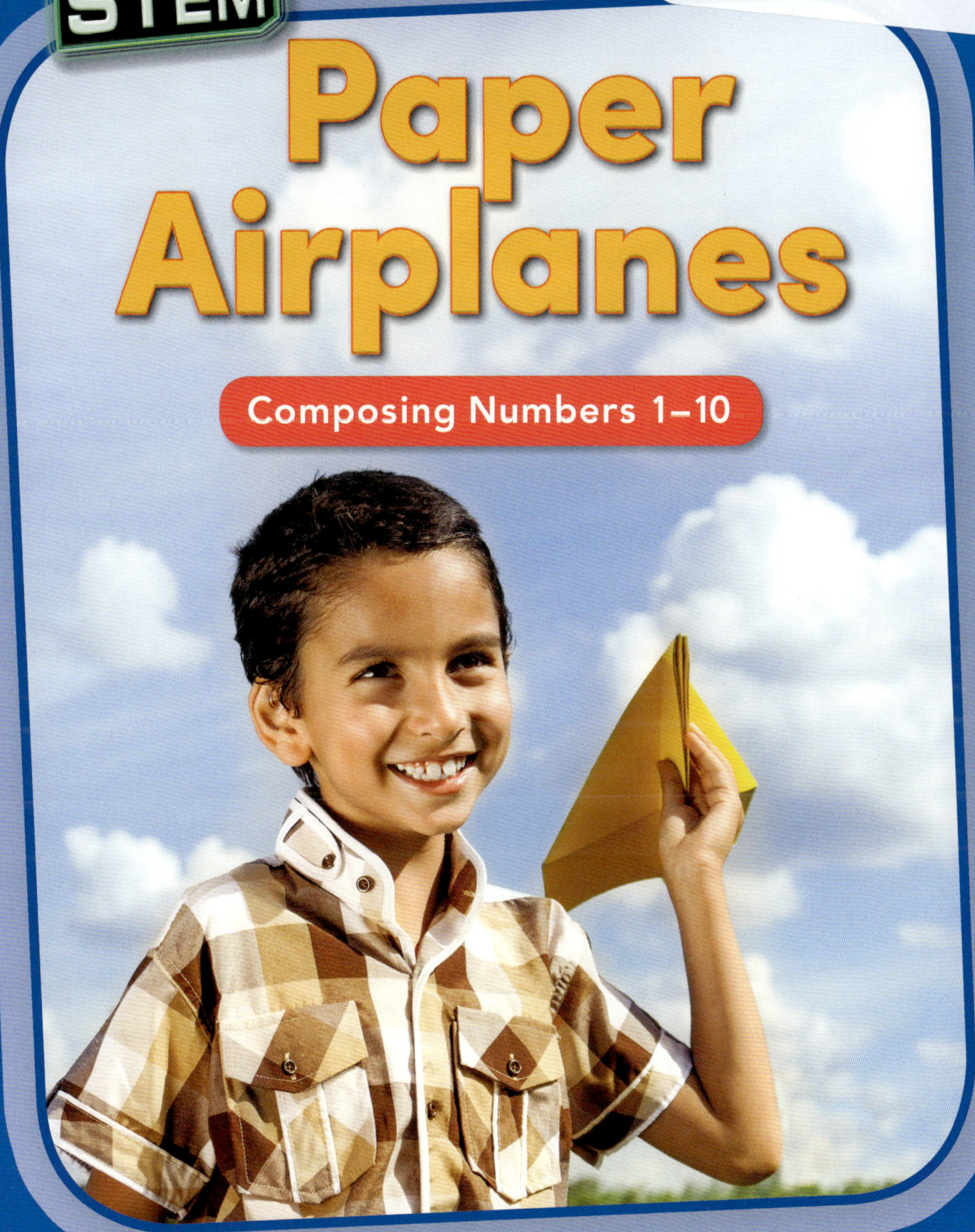

Logan Avery

1 airplane loops.

2 airplanes glide.

3 airplanes spin.

4 airplanes crash.

5 airplanes dip.

6 airplanes fly.

7 airplanes land.

Problem Solving

Jada folds 10 paper airplanes. Some are red and some are blue.

1. How many of each color could she have? Use objects or draw pictures to solve.

2. How many ways can you solve the problem?

Answer Key

1. Answers will vary.
   Examples:
   2 red and 8 blue;
   5 red and 5 blue;
   8 red and 2 blue

2. Answers will vary but should show that there is more than 1 way to solve.

Consultants

Nicole Belasco, M.Ed.
Kindergarten Teacher, Colonial School District

Colleen Pollitt, M.A.Ed.
Math Support Teacher, Howard County Public Schools

Publishing Credits

Rachelle Cracchiolo, M.S.Ed., *Publisher*
Conni Medina, M.A.Ed., *Managing Editor*
Dona Herweck Rice, *Series Developer*
Emily R. Smith, M.A.Ed., *Series Developer*
Diana Kenney, M.A.Ed., NBCT, *Content Director*
June Kikuchi, *Content Director*
Véronique Bos, *Creative Director*
Robin Erickson, *Art Director*
Stacy Monsman, M.A., and Karen Malaska, M.Ed., *Editors*
Michelle Jovin, M.A., *Associate Editor*
Fabiola Sepulveda, *Graphic Designer*

Image Credits: All images from iStock and/or Shutterstock.

Library of Congress Cataloging-in-Publication Data

Names: Avery, Logan, author.
Title: STEM. Paper airplanes / Logan Avery.
Other titles: Paper airplanes
Description: Huntington Beach, CA : Teacher Created Materials, Inc., [2018] | Audience: Grades K to 3.
Identifiers: LCCN 2017059901 (print) | LCCN 2018012058 (ebook) | ISBN 9781480759619 (e-book) | ISBN 9781425856236 (pbk.)
Subjects: LCSH: Paper airplanes--Juvenile literature. | Aerodynamics--Juvenile literature.
Classification: LCC TL778 (ebook) | LCC TL778 .A94 2018 (print) | DDC 745.592--dc23
LC record available at https://lccn.loc.gov/2017059901

Teacher Created Materials
5301 Oceanus Drive
Huntington Beach, CA 92649-1030
www.tcmpub.com

ISBN 978-1-4258-5623-6

Printed by: 51497
Printed in: China